# Star SCENE

# JUST JONAS!

## The Jonas Brothers Up Close and Personal

JOE

KEVIN

NICK

## By Michael-Anne Johns

Scholastic Inc.

New York    Toronto    London    Auckland    Sydney

Mexico City    New Delhi    Hong Kong    Buenos Aires

# PHOTO CREDITS

**Front cover:** Anthony Cutajar/ Retna. **Back cover:** Frazer Harrison/Getty Images. **Page 1:** (Left) Kevin Parry/WireImage.com; (center) Kristin Callahan/Everett Collection; (right) Jason Kempin/FilmMagic.com. **Page 4:** Jason Kempin/FilmMagic.com. **Page 6:** Michael Germana/Everett Collection. **Page 7:** AP Photo/Jason DeCrow. **Page 8:** Lisa O'Connor/ZUMA/Corbis. **Page 9:** Michael Loccisano/FilmMagic.com. **Page 10:** (Top) Jeff Kravitz/FilmMagic.com; (bottom) AP Photo/Hard Rock Cafe, Aynsley Floyd. **Page 11:** (Top) AP Photo/Hard Rock Cafe, Aynsley Floyd; (bottom) Jeff Kravitz/FilmMagic.com. **Page 12:** Anthony Cutajar / Retna Ltd. **Page 13:** Anthony Cutajar/Retna Ltd. **Page 14:** Jason Kempin/FilmMagic.com. **Page 16:** Kevin Parry/ WireImage/Getty Images. **Page 18:** Anthony Cutajar/Retna Ltd. **Page 19:** Reuters/Mario Anzuoni. **Page 21:** Kevin Winter/Getty Images. **Page 22:** Anthony Cutajar/Retna Ltd. **Page 23:** Anthony Cutajar/Retna Ltd. **Page 24:** Kevin Parry/WireImage/Getty Images. **Page 25:** Anthony Cutajar/Retna Ltd. **Page 26:** Anthony Cutajar/Retna Ltd. **Page 27:** Michael Germana/Everett Collection. **Page 28:** Anthony Cutajar/Retna Ltd. **Page 30:** AP Photo/Tammie Arroyo. **Page 33:** AP Photo/Luis Martinez. **Page 34:** Jeff Kravitz/FilmMagic.com. **Page 36:** Anthony Cutajar/Retna Ltd. **Page 38:** Anthony Cutajar/Retna Ltd. **Page 42:** Fernando Leon/Retna Ltd. **Page 43:** AP Photo/Jennifer Graylock. **Page 44:** Anthony Cutajar/ Retna Ltd. **Page 45:** Mathew Imaging/FilmMagic.com. **Page 46:** Anthony Cutajar/ Retna Ltd. **Page 47:** Frank Micelotta/Fox/Getty Images. **Page 48:** Jeff Kravitz/Variety via FilmMagic.com.

ISBN-10: 0-545-08343-5
ISBN-13: 978-0-545-08343-0

Published by Scholastic Inc.
SCHOLASTIC and associated logos are trademarks and/or registered trademarks of Scholastic Inc.

Copyright © 2008 Scholastic Inc.
12 11 10 9 8 7 6 5 4 3 2 1      8 9 10 11 12 /0

Designed by Angela Jun
Printed in the U.S.A.
First printing, April 2008

# CONTENTS

# KEVIN JONAS!
# JOSEPH JONAS!
# NICHOLAS JONAS!

You can almost hear the roar of cheers from the Jonas Brothers fans when you just say their names. Not since Hanson, and before them the Jackson Five, have brothers made music lovers jump to their feet, sing along, and dance, dance, dance.

Though the Jonas Brothers were off to a slow start in 2005 and 2006 when they first appeared on the scene and released their debut CD, *It's About Time*, things definitely changed in 2007. They changed record labels, yes, but that wasn't all. The Jonas Brothers' die-hard fans stuck with Kevin, Joe, and Nick. Even when the guys didn't have a single out on the charts, their Jonas-ites were demanding information about them — from fan blogs and chat rooms, fan sites, and, most important, the teen fan magazines. Kevin, Joe, and Nick were constant cover guys in the magazines. Interviews with the Jonas siblings were worth their weight in gold!

Well, that means the following pages might help solve the national debt — you'll find all the interviews, quotes, facts, fun, and pinups you ever could want. So read on and get ready for a Jonas-good time!

## THE ROAD TO SUCCESS

Up until 2005, the small township of Wyckoff in northeastern New Jersey was best known as a friendly community where every one of the 16,000 population was known as a "neighbor." Wyckoff's known as the "Garden Town" of the Garden State, and the beautiful tree-lined community lives up to it. Little did the residents know there was a hurricane coming — not of the weather kind, but of the musical kind!

# THE JONAS BROTHERS BUZZ

Hurricane Jonas — Joe, Kevin, and Nick Jonas — appeared on the musical Doppler reports in the year 2005. But music was part of the Jonas family's life way before that! The brothers' parents, Kevin, Sr. and Denise Jonas, belonged to a singing group that often traveled the East Coast to perform at small venues. So, back in Wyckoff, the soundtrack of the Jonas household was constantly playing. For as long as they can remember, Kevin, Joe, and Nick were singing, playing musical instruments, even writing lyrics, but it was Nick who first made the professional move.

Legend says that Nick was singing in a barbershop in Wyckoff and was discovered by a music manager. Soon the six-year-old Nick was commuting from Wyckoff to New York City — he was appearing on Broadway in such mega hits as *Beauty and the Beast, A Christmas Carol, Les Misérables, Annie Get Your Gun,* and *The Sound of Music.* Then, when Nick was nine years old, he and his dad worked together on a song, "Joy to the World (A Christmas Prayer)," which was included on the 2002 annual Broadway *Equity Fights AIDS* album, *Broadway's Greatest Gifts: Carols for a Cure Vol. 4.* Kevin, Sr. sang on the CD, but Nick had made a demo of the song, and it came to the attention of Steve Greenberg, who was then the president of Columbia Records. It just so happens that Greenberg also was the man who discovered the powerhouse sibling group Hanson, so his "ear" was tuned to chart-toppers.

# JONAS BROTHERS HIT THE BIG TIME

Initially, Greenberg was interested in signing Nick as a solo act, but then he found out that Nick's older brothers, Kevin, and Joe, had co-written songs on the demo CD. When the boys paid a visit to Columbia's Madison Avenue offices in NYC, they sang "Please Be Mine." Greenberg signed the boys, as a group, immediately!

Kevin, Joe, and Nick headed into the studio to work on their debut CD, *It's About Time*. The transformation was amazing. Initially, Nick had been a Broadway singer, and the first songs written for the demo CD had been Christian rock. Now the guys were creating a punk-pop CD. With a huge fanbase already tuning into the guys via MySpace, it looked like *It's About Time* would be an instant hit.

The first single, "Mandy" did make MTV-*TRL* history. The song was about a girl that Joseph used to date. Though they were no longer seeing each other romantically, she remained friends with the entire Jonas family. Actually, Joseph recalls, "She was Nick's best friend when they were little. But she got older and I guess I saw something in her differently and we started dating. And it was really cool, but it didn't work out. We're still like the best of friends."

"Mandy" was the Jonas Brothers' first video and they filmed it as a three-part story, each of which was released consecutively on TRL. Shortly after that, Jonas Brothers songs began appearing on TV shows and soundtracks — "Time For Me to Fly" on the *Aquamarine* soundtrack, "Mandy" featured on *Zoey 101: Spring Break-Up*, the theme song of *American Dragon: Jake Long*, and many more.

# JONAS TIME

**O**n June 25, 2007, the Jonas Brothers headed out on a three-month U.S. tour. They performed at large theaters, small clubs, fairgrounds, and the like. It was like a family road trip because the boys' parents and their little six-year-old brother, Frankie, joined them on the tour buses.

The tour was leading up to some major Jonas Brothers events. On August 7, their CD, *Jonas Brothers*, was released. To celebrate the day, Nick says, "Our dad rented a yacht the night our album came out. We sailed to the Statue of Liberty. It was a blast."

On August 17, they appeared on the "Me and Mr. Jonas and Mr. Jonas and Mr. Jonas" episode of *Hannah Montana*.

In the following months, they performed on TV shows, won awards, and on October 18, they headed out on a 54-date concert tour with Miley Cyrus.

Now the Jonas Brothers are part of the Disney family, and using the super success of *Jonas Brothers* as a springboard, they put "taking breaks" behind them. Just as they wound up the Miley Cyrus tour in January 2008, Kevin, Joe, and Nick were scheduled to head into production of a live-action spy comedy for Disney. It's called *J.O.N.A.S.*, and it's about three brothers who are special agents for the government — Junior Operatives Networking as Spies. They are undercover as a hit rock band, but when they aren't performing, they are super spies!

"It's exciting!" Kevin told a reporter. And he was pleased because the producers of *J.O.N.A.S.* treated them with as much respect as did the Hollywood Records folks. "With the script, they're very open with us," he explained. "If we were, like, 'I would never, ever say that line,' you know, [they'd change it]."

"The characters are us," adds Nick, "so they kind of have to fit our personalities. We got time to meet the writers so they got to know who we are. It was cool."

With all this happening, it really looks as if it's Jonas Time . . . and it's about time!

# MUSICAL NOTES

MUSICAL NOTES

## THE JONAS MELODY OF LIFE

**Singing is my life . . .** *I think I have always known that. It's just something that since I can remember, I knew. That is something that everybody always says, but for me it is true. From the age of two, I was telling my grandma I had to practice because I was going to be on Broadway.* — Nick

**The first song I remember singing . . .** *was probably a song from Peter Pan. I used to watch that every day, I know "Neverland," that song, " I know a place where dreams are born . . ." That is the song I sang.* — Nick

**I think I always wanted to make people laugh . . .** *That is my job — to be a comedian all day. I loved the show All That, and when I was younger I always watched it. I was like, "One day I am going to be on that stage and make people laugh." Then when I was singing around the house my dad was like, "Joe you have a great voice and you should sing." I was like, "You know, OK." I love what we are doing right now. People love it and it is really cool.* — Joe

ROCK

10

**Jonas Brothers is . . .** *the album of our dreams. We're getting to make the music from scratch — from the drums to the bass to the guitar to the vocals. We're picking songs that we want to be on the record and we're all playing and singing, so we're really excited because this is the album that we really wanted to make. It's also exciting because this is the first record we made that I really, really enjoy listening to on my iPod. — Kevin*

**Jonas Brothers is . . .** *just the Jonas Brothers being the Jonas Brothers, which we think is really cool. We create the music that we want to create and people enjoy it, so it's awesome. — Nick*

**Jonas Brothers is . . .** *just us, updated. — Joe*

**We get our song inspirations . . .** *from a lot of different places. A lot are from personal experiences. — Nick*

**Little brother, Frankie . . .** *says he kind of wants to make his own band. He hasn't warmed up to the idea of being in our band. — Joe*

**My musical inspiration is** . . . my dad. He was so good. We were always playing [music] around the house. — *Kevin*

**We grew up listening to** . . . old-school music. Some of our favorite musicians are the Beatles and Switchfoot. — *Joe*

**I've always described our sound** . . . as music on Red Bull! — *Kevin*

**Writing together** . . . feels like the most natural thing we could be doing. When we write a song, we get in a triangle. I start playing the chords that we've chosen over and over, and then we'll keep going around in a circle until we have figured out the lyrics for the song. — *Kevin*

**Nick is** . . . the powerhouse vocal. He's just got this young, soulful voice that catches everyone's ear. — *Joe*

**Joe just has** . . . this really cool, smooth rock voice. He really knows how to get the crowd going. — *Nick*

**Kevin is** . . . the one that holds us all together. Joseph and I are the singers and take turns on keyboards and percussion, but Kevin mostly plays the guitar and that's the part of the group that we need — he's the glue that keeps us together. — *Nick*

**Our fans . . .** *are awesome! They're more like our friends. We start recognizing people, too, especially on our MySpace. —* *Joe*

**Music is . . .** *like my life. I guess music to me is very special. You have to have music [to express your] feelings — every time that you are happy, you can, like, put it into a song. There are songs when you are happy, and there are songs when you are sad. It is just everyday things like that. —* *Joe*

**Music is . . .** *like life in general. When you walk outside, you know, you hear things and especially when you are in the studio a lot of times, you start hearing beats with everything you do. Everything becomes a song, and that is really how our life has become. —* *Kevin*

## DISCOGRAPHY

### Albums

- *It's About Time*
  (Columbia Records) August 8, 2006

- *Jonas Brothers*
  (Hollywood Records) August 7, 2007

- *Jonas Brothers: Bonus Jonas Edition*
  (Hollywood Records) October 30, 2007

### Singles

- "Mandy" — *Zoey 101: Music Mix* and *It's About Time*
- "Year 3000" — *It's About Time* and *Jonas Brothers*
- "Poor Unfortunate Souls" — *Disney's Little Mermaid Special Edition* soundtrack
- "Kids of the Future" — *Meet The Robinsons* soundtrack and *Jonas Brothers*
- "Hold On" — *Jonas Brothers*
- "S.O.S." — *Jonas Brothers*

KIDS OF THE FUTURE
MANDY
JUST FRIENDS
S.O.S.
GOODNIGHT, GOODBYE
HELLO
AUSTRALIA
AIN'T NO SUNSHINE...
THAT'S JUST THE WAY WE ROLL
HOLLYWOOD
INSEPARABLE
STILL IN LOVE
HOLD ON
YEAR 3000

JONAS BROTHERS

# SPOTLIGHT ON KEVIN

Kevin Jonas is known as Mr. Charm; he has the charisma and smooth appeal that attracts millions of fans. Besides being a guitar hero, Kevin is the grounding force of the sibling trio. Nick has called him "the glue" that keeps the group together. Nick and Joe often look to Kevin to keep things level and reasonable in a world where life could be pretty chaotic.

Kevin knows how to treat people, especially girls. He's always a gentleman. For example, he recently told a teen magazine reporter, "I think guys should still open a door for a girl every chance they get, every time. They should try to take care of a girl as much as possible. She's like a princess, no matter what."

Well, believe it or not, there's another side to Kevin. While a lot of people think he's King of Hearts, Kevin is the first to admit that he isn't always perfect.

"I've always been scared of failing," he confesses. "I hate to disappoint those I care about — I want to make them happy. I'm such a people-pleaser, especially in relationships. I'm definitely working on it. I try not to be a push-over, and I'm really making an effort to voice my opinion more."

When it comes to girls, well, Kev doesn't have the "I can date anyone" attitude. "I'm afraid of getting rejected by girls," he admits. "And rejection can be the worst in music. I have to remind myself that although it may be risky, I'm doing what I love. I also know that if you don't take chances, then you'll never know what will happen!"

## KEVIN TIDBITS

- Kevin has a collection of guitars and other musical instruments, including four acoustic guitars, six electric guitars, one bass guitar, and two drum sets.
- One of Kevin's acoustic guitars was handmade. The wood is from Africa and is very rare.
- Kevin admits he thinks *High School Musical*'s Ashley Tisdale is awesome!
- Kevin is a neat freak — "I hate not having clean clothes. If I have a shirt and I wore it, it needs to be cleaned. I'm really weird about it."
- Kevin's fave tech toy is his iPhone!

# SPOTLIGHT ON JOE

According to his mom, Denise: "Joe is just quiet, very sweet, but he has a mischievous side. When he was little, he had an adorable face, big brown eyes and puffy hair. . . . Joseph was very attached to his Barney, and I was like, we have to get rid of this thing. I had my friend bring it to the trash and Joseph saw her. He said, 'Why do you have my Barney?'"

Well, that was then, this is now . . . Joe's Barney is long gone, and he's dealing with the "shy" side of his personality.

"It used to bother me that I was shy," he says. "I was always the one playing it safe, never coming out of my shell because I was afraid. I've since grown up — I'm outgoing, and I just like to have fun!"

But some things never change. Joe may have been traumatized by the puffy hair thing, because he admits, "I tend to worry about how I look! It's good that I have my brothers around to reassure me. If they weren't there, I probably wouldn't get out of the bed in the morning! I'm also always checking the mirror because I'm afraid that I have something in my teeth. It's an insecurity!"

## JUMPIN' JOE

- Napoleon Dynamite is the kind of movie that makes Joe laugh.
- Joe's mom recalls one early romantic gesture — "He bought this girl he likes a pretty little stone that said something on it and put it in a heart box and gave it to her. She rejected him!"
- Joe's nickname is Danger.
- Joe loves girls with accents!
- If Joe were president, he would make sure "I'd have a fresh pair of socks every day!"

# SPOTLIGHT ON NICK

Though the Jonas Brothers are the hottest band around today, life isn't always picture-perfect. Sure they have to deal with adult problems that other teens don't, but one day Nick came up against a challenge that could have been life-or-death.

In the fall of 2005, the guys were on tour, preparing the way for the release of their first CD, *It's About Time*. It was a long, stressful tour, but Nick, who is usually the Energizer Bunny, began feeling tired, listless, and moody.

"I started experiencing weight loss, a bad attitude — things that weren't me," he recalls. "So after the tour we went to the doctor and found out I had diabetes. The first thing I asked the doctor was if I was going to die. It was crazy."

Not so crazy — Type 1 Diabetes is a major concern with kids in the U.S. today, and if undetected, it could cause all sorts of medical and physical problems. When diagnosed, the disease requires constant vigilance — daily insulin injections, careful diet, exercise, and regular visits to the doctor.

Nick had to spend three days in the hospital to get himself on the right track, and during that time he learned about the disease — and how to live with it. "It was hard," he says. "There were times I just didn't want to have it. It was a learning process."

One lucky medical advance Nick has taken advantage of is something called the OmniPod. It is a pump that is attached to his skin that constantly drips insulin into his body, so he doesn't need to give himself shots.

Because Nick realized so many kids across the country are also living with Type 1 Diabetes, he and his family decided he was going to go public about his illness. So at a concert at the Diabetes Research Institute's Carnival for a Cure, Nick made the announcement, and ever since then, he has worked hard to get the message out — deal with the disease and learn to live your life to the fullest!

## NICK'S QUICKIES

- Nick loves to listen to Johnny Cash.
- Nick loves the word "Excellent!"
- Nick thinks Corbin Bleu's Chad was the coolest character in *High School Musical*.
- Nick hates it when someone pretends to be him on MySpace.
- Nick loves that designers give the group clothes — "Free clothes! I haven't actually purchased any clothes in about a year. We're blessed!"

"OUR FANS ARE AMAZING. THEY'LL DRIVE ACROSS THE COUNTRY, STAND OUTSIDE UNTIL WHO KNOWS WHEN. WE APPRECIATE EVERYTHING THE FANS DO." — *Kevin*

"WE ARE HAVING A GREAT TIME DOING THIS. WE LIKE TO SEE PEOPLE ENJOYING OUR MUSIC AND HAVING FUN AT OUR CONCERTS" — *Joe*

"WE TAKE TIME TO MEET EVERY SINGLE ONE OF OUR FANS IF WE CAN. WE LOVE OUR FANS AND WOULD BE NOWHERE WITHOUT THEM." — *Nick*

"WHEN WE'RE SITTING AT HOME, WE DON'T WANT TO BE THERE. WE WANT TO BE OUT PLAYING OR WRITING SONGS. THIS IS WHAT WE WANT TO DO." — *Kevin*

"BEFORE A CONCERT, WE HAVE A 45-MINUTE LOCKDOWN WHERE NO ONE LEAVES AND NO ONE COMES IN. WE GET READY FOR THE SHOW, WE CHANGE, GET FOCUSED, PLAY THROUGH ALL OF THE SONGS FOR THAT NIGHT ON THE ACOUSTIC GUITAR, DO VOCALS, PRAY, DO PUSH UPS, EAT FOOD."
— *Kevin*

"THERE'S NO JEALOUSY—I THINK WE'RE GOOD ABOUT THAT; WE'VE BEEN DOING THIS FOR A WHILE NOW AND IT'S NOT AN ISSUE. OUR PARENTS ARE AMAZING; PEOPLE AROUND US ARE AMAZING. [WE ALSO KEEP] EACH OTHER IN CHECK—THAT'S REALLY IMPORTANT." — *Nick*

# THE ULTIMATE JONAS Q&A

**ARE YOUR FRIENDS SURPRISED BY WHAT IS HAPPENING TO YOU GUYS?**

**Joe:** Yeah, it is pretty crazy. It is weird sometimes, but we love it when we walk into our local Starbucks in our town. We can easily go hang out, and then we get stopped about three or four times by, like, nobody that we know.

**Kevin:** People who we used to go to school with come up and say, "Hey, you guys have a ringtone." We are like "Yeah, we do," and that is really strange.

**Joe:** They are looking through their phone and are like, "Wait . . . The Jonas Brothers . . . 'Mandy'. I went to school with them!"

**NOW THAT YOU ARE WITH HOLLYWOOD RECORDS, YOU HAVE MOVED OUT TO LOS ANGELES — DO YOU LIKE IT?**

**Nick:** Yeah. We rented a house to stay in while we're recording the new album, and it's so much fun.

**WHAT DO YOU LIKE BEST ABOUT LOS ANGELES?**

**Kevin:** The weather — it's 75 degrees even in February. That's nice. You can go swimming all year round. The people are really cool. It's a lot of fun.

**WHAT DO YOU MISS MOST ABOUT NEW JERSEY?**

**Nick:** We'll be back there all the time, so hopefully we won't miss it too much while we're out here. We'll be [back] there soon enough.

**Joe:** One thing they don't have out here [in L.A.] is Rita's Italian Ices. We used to have one right next to our house and it was so good.

**WHAT'S THE SILLIEST STORY YOU'VE SEEN WRITTEN ABOUT YOU?**

**Kevin:** There was one that said I was married. I was like, "No, no, that didn't happen."

**Nick:** There was one that said that I was shy, which I'm not, I just don't talk as much as my brothers.

**WHAT'S THE SILLIEST QUESTION YOU'VE EVER BEEN ASKED BY AN INTERVIEWER?**

**Joe:** "What do you think about scoliosis?" We kind of answered like, "Well, I know it's not good. You should probably get it checked out."

**DO YOU PREFER ANY ONE TYPE OF VENUE — CLUB, STADIUM, ARENA — OVER ANOTHER?**

**Nick:** I definitely like to mix it up. We can play a huge arena, and then we can go to a small, 100-person show in a little theater. It's cool to mix it up. Of course, big is nice, but it's all fun.

**DO YOU GUYS STILL USE THE INTERNET FOR GRASSROOTS SUPPORT AS YOU DID IN YOUR EARLY CAREER?**

**Joe:** Totally. Every single day, we're on MySpace talking to fans. They sometimes use crazy online lingo that we can't understand, but my dad's the best when he reads them to us. He'll say, "Yo, you guys are hot." So we do it every day, and we like to keep doing it ourselves. We like to go online and write to the fans ourselves, and go on the chat boards and talk to fans and get to know them. It's just awesome.

## WHAT'S THE FUNNIEST FAN EXPERIENCE YOU'VE EVER HAD?

**Kevin:** There's been so many. I don't know.

**Joe:** When we were in Nashville, we came from a long day of interviews. It was midnight. And we stayed in this motel because every other hotel was booked since there was a big award show that night. So we pulled up and we were so excited to go to bed, but all of a sudden this car screeches up to us. The window rolls down, and this older lady looks at us and says, "We wanted to find you." I just looked at my dad and was like, "What's going on?" And they asked if they could take a picture and we said sure. And then they said, "Don't worry, we won't come to your rooms. But we know you're staying in 816 and 817. We've been sitting here for two hours." So we went inside and we told the manager to change our rooms. It was so funny. I thought we were going to die that day! Another one is when we went to one school and I don't know why, but the girls would cry. I was like, "Why would they cry?"

**Kevin:** Just to meet us. They were banging on the door screaming . . .

**Joe:** . . . like for an hour-and-a-half and one girl was crying. Skipping school just to meet us.

**Kevin:** She got suspended. We actually have this one fan from North Carolina. We have been doing shows [all over], and she has actually been flying to our shows.

**Joe:** She has actually been driving sometimes.

**Kevin:** She drove twelve hours [one] day . . .

**Joe:** . . . just to see us, so we actually brought her onstage and sang her a song. She loved it. She thought it was the greatest thing.

**Kevin:** It made her day.

## DO YOU HAVE ANY SPECIFIC FEARS OR PHOBIAS?

**Joe:** I'm afraid that when I'm asleep that somebody might want to break into my house and punch me. It's called the Afraidthatpeoplearegoingtopunchyouphobia.

**Kevin:** It's more about feeling like you disappoint people — that's the fear I have.

**Nick:** We've gotten this question a lot, but I don't know if I'm afraid of anything. Maybe of not succeeding — but that's more of a doubt than a fear.

## HAVE ANY OF YOU READ A BOOK IN THIS PAST YEAR THAT YOU WOULD LIKE TO RECOMMEND?

**Nick:** I've started on the whole *Chronicles of Narnia* series. It's really, really good. . . . But I have always loved the *Magic Tree House* books. They are my favorite. I still read them. That lets you know how much I love them. I started reading them when I was in third grade.

**Kevin:** I definitely agree with Nick. *The Chronicles of Narnia* books are great books. I've been reading them after not having read them since middle school . . . it opens your eyes to a whole other aspect of it.

**Joe:** I would have to say *A Wrinkle in Time*.

## PART OF THE JONAS BROTHERS LEGEND IS THAT KEVIN LEARNED HOW TO PLAY THE GUITAR BY READING A BOOK CALLED *TEACH YOURSELF HOW TO PLAY GUITAR.* THE STORY WAS IN YOUR ORIGINAL BIO — IS IT TRUE?

**Kevin:** Yes! I actually faked sick that next day so I could stay home and continue learning. They left that part out of the bio. Yeah, I mean Nick actually plays drums. We both play guitar and piano, so we do that in our set when we do it live and stuff which is really cool. I have plenty of instruments. My parents are very musical. They are always teaching me new things. We have a piano in the house and guitars. We have tons of guitars, and so it is very cool that we get to just write songs.

## DO YOU HAVE ALL-TIME FAVORITE SONGS?

**Kevin:** It may have to be "3x5" by John Mayer. There is a line that says "There is no 3x5 this time because I want to see the world though both my eyes," and I had to think about it. [I wondered] "What does he mean by that?" And then I realized that if you have to take a picture then you have to close one of your eyes to actually take a picture, and he just wanted to take it all in. I was like, "Whoa that is awesome." It was one of those songs that made me think and really inspired me and the way that I write songs.

**Joe:** Switchfoot, they have a song. I think "Only Hope" is what it is called. I love Switchfoot, and I love that song. It is really cool.

**Nick:** My all-time favorite song would have to be "Superstition" by Stevie Wonder. I love that song. It is so good. I bought a new cell phone the other week, and the first thing I did was bought the ringtone for "Superstition."

**YOU ARE ON THE ROAD A GOOD PART OF THE YEAR — IS THAT HARD ON YOU GUYS?**

**Kevin:** Wow, I love it. It is so great. I get to travel the world and do music. It is so cool. This year I got to see a lot of the U.S. I think my three top favorite places are L.A., Boston, and New York.

**Joe:** Yeah, same for me from what I have seen so far. Yeah, they are beautiful places.

**Kevin:** I really enjoyed Boston. It was a great town. Every time we have been able to go we have actually been able to go and hang out downtown for a while.

**Joe:** I was like, "I did not know that Harvard was in Boston." When I saw it I was like, "Whoa, it is huge."

**WHEN YOU FIRST STARTED AND WENT ON TOUR, YOU TRAVELED BY CAR — WHO DROVE?**

**Kevin:** We are all backseat drivers. . . . Joseph and Nicholas are the worst backseat drivers. They are like, "Slow down, slow down!" And I will be like, "I am going the speed limit, leave me alone." They are so bad.

**ARE YOU GUYS GOOD AT READING MAPS? DO YOU GET LOST?**

**Joe:** Oh, yeah, we get lost!

**Kevin:** We have to count every day how many U-turns we take. It is bad.

**Joe:** There was one time when we were coming home from a show and we were going to go out to eat and we are [looking for] a nice restaurant. You know, when you go on tour you have to make [the best of] what you got to eat because you [usually end up going to] McDonald's. So we drove I think two hours away from our hotel by accident. It was pretty funny. It was pretty bad. We were on the road and we all fell asleep and we wake up and we were still in the same place. They said we had to turn around and we drove like halfway there and halfway back.

**YOU GUYS HAVE BEEN QUOTED THAT A GUY NAMED "JOEY BAG OF DONUTS" IS ONE OF YOUR BEST FRIENDS — WHO IS THAT?**

**Joe:** That is his nickname.

**Kevin:** It was so great because he actually flew out for the shoot of our first video. He is this Hollister, Abercrombie kind of kid. He is big with blond hair and blue eyes, and he just looks like a total surf dude.

**Joe:** He flew out, and he ended up being one of the main character bullies in the "Mandy" video.

**Q: HOW DO YOU GUYS SETTLE YOUR DIFFERENCES?**

**Kevin:** Sometimes there is the awkward moment when you are just like, "Oh, whatever."

**Joe:** We're brothers, and we are always going to have some quarrels. Nick always gets upset if I wear his socks. He always gets upset and freaks out and he is like, "Joey, you were in my dresser."

**Kevin:** I mean, we usually just get along. We get along pretty well because we are also a band. We know we can't just get upset [with] each other and hold grudges while you are on stage. It is not going to work. We know how to work it out. We know things are petty and we are just like, "You know forget it."

**Q: IF YOU WEREN'T INTO MUSIC WHAT DO YOU THINK YOU WOULD LIKE TO PURSUE?**

**Nick:** Sports. I am a sports fanatic. I love sports. I think I am probably one of the biggest Yankees fans alive.

**Q: HOW MANY YANKEE GAMES HAVE YOU SEEN?**

**Nick:** Oh, this is the best part. Check this out, I don't go to very many games, but I watch every single game on TV, every single one. So I am pretty crazy about the Yankees. When I can't actually watch it live, I TiVo it. . . . I am also a die hard Dallas Cowboys fan. I don't tell many people that because I will get made fun of.

**WHAT ARE YOU MOST LOOKING FORWARD TO OVER THE NEXT YEAR?**

**Nick:** I am really looking forward to how this whole thing is going to unfold. I truly believe that this [CD] is going to be a success and a great record that people will really enjoy. I just can't wait — people have been waiting for it to come out for so long. I am excited to see my dreams come true. I am excited to do what I love.

# KEVIN'S FACT SHEET

## FACTS

**FULL NAME:** Paul Kevin Jonas II

**NICKNAME:** (Who gave it to you & why) don't have one

**BIRTHDATE:** 11/5/87

**BIRTHPLACE:** Teaneck, New Jersey

**CURRENT RESIDENCE:** Hollywood, CA

**RIGHTY OR LEFTY?** Righty

**HEIGHT:** 5'11"

**WEIGHT:** 135 lb

**HAIR & EYE COLOR:** brown & hazel

**PARENTS:** Kevin and Denise

**CHILDHOOD PETS:** Cocco (dog)

**BEST FRIENDS:** John Taylor

**DESCRIBE YOURSELF AS A CHILD:** Super hyper

## DATING

**GIRLFRIEND/BOYFRIEND:** Girlfriend

**MOST ROMANTIC DATE:** Gentlemen don't kiss and tell

**TURN ON:** love a girl with good style

**FIRST DATE:** was great

**WORST DATE?** haven't had one yet

**WHAT MAKES YOU ASK FOR/WANT TO GO ON A SECOND DATE?**
if I had a really good time

**DO YOU LIKE A GIRL TO ASK YOU OUT?(FOR BOYS):** No!

**WHAT WOULD YOU BUY A GIRLFRIEND/BOYFRIEND FOR HER/HIS BIRTHDAY?**
Jewelry

**EVER DATE A FAN?** If I get to know her/yes but always looking.

## FIRST

**KISS:** don't kiss and tell

**THEME PARK VISIT:** Disneyland

**MOVIE:** Jungle Book

**CONCERT:** Mxpx

**CD/ALBUM BOUGHT:** Mxpx

**MAJOR PURCHASE** Jeep

**CAR:** Toyota Camry

**GIRLFRIEND/BOYFRIEND:** can't remember

# JOE'S FACT SHEET

## FACTS

**FULL NAME:** Joseph Adam Jonas

**NICKNAME:** (Who gave it to you & why) Danger—because I'm crazy

**BIRTHDATE:** 8/15/89

**BIRTHPLACE:** Arizona

**CURRENT RESIDENCE:** California

**RIGHTY OR LEFTY?** Righty

**HEIGHT:** 5'8"

**WEIGHT:** 140 lb

**HAIR & EYE COLOR:** black & brown

**PARENTS:** Denise and Kevin Jonas

**CHILDHOOD PETS:** Cocco (dog)

**BEST FRIENDS:** Amelia

**DESCRIBE YOURSELF AS A CHILD:** amazing, funny, adorable

# FIRST

**KISS:** was great!

**THEME PARK VISIT:** Six Flags Over Texas

**MOVIE:** Homeward Bound

**CONCERT:** Kenny G.

**CD/ALBUM BOUGHT:** Britney Spears

**MAJOR PURCHASE:** Nike Dunks

**CAR:** can't drive yet

# SCHOOL STUFF

**BEST/FAVE SUBJECT—WHY?** math-because I like to challenge myself

**FAVE TEACHER—WHY?** John Taylor—he's helpful

**DO YOU FIND MATH EASY/HARD?** hard

**ANY MATH TIPS?** don't forget your calculator

**SCIENCE DISASTER:** I once broke 2 beakers on the floor

**DID YOU LIKE HISTORY?** no. . . I love it

**WHAT HISTORICAL ERA WOULD YOU LIKE TO VISIT? WHY?** the 80's-good music, great food

**MOST EMBARRASSING MOMENTS IN SCHOOL:** getting called to the principal's office the first day of the new year

# NICK'S FACT SHEET

## FACTS

**FULL NAME:** Nicholas Jerry Jonas

**BIRTHDATE:** 9/16/92

**BIRTHPLACE:** Dallas, Texas

**CURRENT RESIDENCE:** California

**RIGHTY OR LEFTY?** Righty

**HEIGHT:** 5' 6"

**WEIGHT:** 105 lb

**HAIR & EYE COLOR:** brown hair and brown eyes

**PARENTS:** Kevin and Denise Jonas

**CHILDHOOD PETS:** Cocco. He's a dog

**BEST FRIENDS:** Maya, Kibble, Mandy, Vandanye

**DESCRIBE YOURSELF AS A CHILD:** very creative and independent. I loved to sing.

# FAVES

**SPORTS:** baseball

**TV SHOWS:** Lost, Sportscenter

**MOVIES:** Finding Neverland and Better off Dead

**ACTOR/ACTRESS:** Jake Long

**BAND/SINGER/MUSICIAN:** Stevie Wonder

**FOOD:** I love steak

**DRINK:** 7-11 Slurpee

**CANDY:** gummy worms

**SANDWICH:** Italian hero

**HOLIDAY—WHY?** Thanksgiving because of all the good food

**FAMILY TRADITION:** Putting up the Christmas tree

# MISC.

**FAVE AFTER SCHOOL SNACK:** Twinkies

**COLLECTIONS:** I collect baseball cards and I have been for the last 3 years

**EVER BEEN IN A FIGHT?** No, sometimes I'll get mad at people but fighting is pointless

**ADVICE ON HOW TO AVOID THEM?** Don't let your temper control your action

**DID YOU EVER SAVE YOUR MONEY OR SPEND IT:** I would save up for a while then I would spend it.

# CRUSHIN' WITH KEV, JOE, & NICK

Love, love, love . . . the Jonas Brothers are definitely all about love! They sing love songs; they love their fans, family, and friends, and, needless to say, they are the most-loved boy band today! Read on for more Jonas details on matters of the heart.

## HALLOWEEN HEARTACHE . . . WELL, STOMACHACHE

Once, Joe had a date on Halloween and he recalls, "I bought this huge costume to make my crush laugh. I was dressed up as a cowboy riding a bull! I liked it because it has this button, when you pressed it, the cowboy suit blew up and became really huge. [My date] was dressed up as a milkshake. It was really awesome! We went trick-or-treating all day. But we ate too much candy, and we both wound up getting sick!"

## LOOKIN' FOR LOVE

"I don't have a girlfriend right now, but I'm always looking," confesses Nick. "I want a girl who understands my crazy schedule, who will be there to support me, and who can make me smile."

## THE SOUND OF LOVE

"For some reason, a girl's voice [attracts me]," admits Joe. "Interesting voices. . . . I like accents, too. Definitely!"

## DREAM GIRL

"Someone that's totally, completely cool," Kevin describes his Ms. Right. "Like, they can just talk to you like we're regular people. I really like it when they're not impressed. Or they put on the face of not being impressed!"

## BUTTERFLIES?
"When I want to ask someone out, I get really excited," says Joe. "Of course, I get a little nervous beforehand, too, you know? But I get more excited than anything else around the girl because I just really want to ask her."

## FIRST MOVE
Kevin knows how to get things going. "I'm a talker, so I talk to people. I'm not afraid to walk up to you and just start talking to you. I won't try to make you laugh, because it's not going to happen — I'm not funny at all."

## NICK'S DREAM DATE:
"I would buy box tickets to a Yankees game and watch the Yankees beat the Red Sox."

## JOE'S DREAM DATE
"It's all about the surprise. I like to have fun, so we'd go bowling."

## KEV'S DREAM DATE
"I believe the best date would be going to New York City and having dinner. A restaurant we like is La Mela. Tables are set up in the street covered with overhanging lights. Then head to a Broadway show. End the date by walking her to the door."

### GIRLS ARE FROM VENUS — BOYS ARE FROM MARS

Nick wants girls to know that there is a big difference between them and how guys look at things. If he could tell girls one thing, it would be, "Guys can't read minds!"

### AN OLD-FASHIONED BOY

"I really love dresses," admits Nick. "I like a girl who looks like a lady."

### THE LOOK

"I'm a sucker for blonds and redheads," spills Kevin. "But sometimes, it's also the smile that gets me."

### THAT CERTAIN SOMETHING

"If [a girl] is talented, that's really cool," Joe says. "Every girl has something special about her. And it's cool if she can share it with everyone! . . . I like girls who like to have fun, too!"

## RUMOR CONTROL

- Joe and AJ Michalka: They did date for a while, but Joe reveals, "It just didn't work out. It was a distance thing."

- Nick and Miley Cyrus: "I am not dating Miley Cyrus," Nick insists. "I mean, yeah, she's pretty, but I didn't date her!"

- Kevin and any girl: "[I] really don't talk about [my] relationship status."

## TURN OFFS:

- "We like good girls," Joe explains. "They can't smoke, and we don't like drugs. . . . Kevin, Nick, and I are in the no-drama zone."

- "If a girl talks about drama at school or her past boyfriend or anything like that, then she's history," maintains Nick.

- "The most annoying thing a girl can do is text on her cell phone during the entire date," says Kevin.

# JONAS BITS & PIECES

## HERE'S A TRIVIA TREASURE TROVE OF KEVIN, JOE, AND NICK!

### COLLECTIONS

Joe used to collect pens. "I don't know why I just always did. I had, like, every pen. . . . It was bad. And then I was like, "Where am I going to put all these pens?'"

Nicholas collects baseball cards. "I have some pretty good ones, too, [but] nothing too great. . . . I have a Barry Bonds rookie card, and that is the one I like. The rest are all kind of like I am waiting for like 25 years to go by so I can have a good card. I know patience. Collecting baseball cards gives you good virtue. Patience and then once you wait a long time it pays off, literally. It pays off."

Kevin isn't much of a collector, but he does have some special action figures. "I have unopened *Star Wars* figures in my attic. Hasbro gave us a special Darth Vadar — when you take off the helmet, it's George Lucas. There are only 100 of them and they gave us three. That was awesome!"

### BABY BOTTLE POPS MANIA

The Jonas Brothers' picture is on the side of the candy Baby Bottle Pops, and Kevin says, "We have them on the tour bus. And they are all over our home. "

### HOME SWEET HOME

There is a wooden sign over the bathroom door at Joe, Kevin, and Nick's New Jersey home that says, "Patience is a virtue!"

## HEARTBREAK

"My favorite song, 'S.O.S.' kicks off the album," says Kevin. "It's fun, but it's also about a girl breaking your heart so bad it feels like you're walking on broken glass."

## OOPS!

Once when the Jonas Brothers were doing a showcase, Joe recalls, "The stage was near the door, so right when you walked out the door you had to jump on the stage. There were tons of wire on the stage. The fans were waiting for us, and they introduced us: 'The Jonas Brothers!' I walked out, and I tripped onto the stage. Nobody really saw it in the back, but everyone in the front row saw it. Somehow I fell backward so I did a 360 and landed on the ground. Someone that works with us onstage was [near me]. I grabbed his shirt and picked myself up. I bowed and I was like, 'Thank you I am here! Did you like that karate move I did?' It was pretty funny!"

## IF YOU COULD CREATE A FLAVOR OF ICE CREAM . . .

"I would invent ice cream that never melts," says Joe. "It would be like space ice cream."

## FOUR!

"Joe and I are in a secret society of golfing," admits Nick. "It's called the Four Kings Golfing Society. It's Joe, me, our guitar player, and our bassist."

## BONUS JONAS

Believe it or not, Kevin, Joe, and Nick's little brother, Frankie, has fans, too. It's been reported that kids have been sighted at Jonas Brothers concerts wearing "I Love Frankie" T-shirts! The guys have nicknamed him "The Bonus Jonas."

## SHARE THE STAGE

Joe says his fantasy tourmates would be amazing. "I would probably shoot for the highest ever. I would say U2 . . . and the Ramones."   Nick adds "Stevie Wonder and Will Smith."

## SHOP TILL YOU DROP

Let the Jonas Brothers loose in a mall and here's what they head for . . .
Kev: . . . jackets and shoes!
Joe: . . . socks and a grill!

## IF I COULD BE AN ANIMAL . . .

Nick: I've been told that I'm most like a wolf.
Kevin: No, you're like a fox.
Nick: A fox?
Kevin: You're sly.
Joe: I've been told I am a fierce lion.
Nick: No! I think you're more like a zebra?
Joe: A zebra?!
Nick: Yeah
Joe: Zebras are cool.
Nick: Kevin is . . .
Joe: A prairie dog!
Kevin: *A WHAT?!*
Nick: I pictured Kevin more like a lizard — an iguana.
All: A gecko!

## FAST FOOD

Joe loves In-N-Out Burger.
Nick is a die-hard McDonald's fan.
Kevin will never turn down a Wendy's grilled chicken sandwich.

## GOBBLE GOBBLE TRADITION

Joe: I don't know what this has to do with traditions, but every time we go into another state we always say "Gobble."

Kevin: We grew up on the road with our parents. They were in a traveling group, and they were singers. They would drive around to different places to perform. When they were on tour, every state line they crossed they would say "Gobble" because it meant one closer city to Thanksgiving break. That is what we do still. Every time we cross a state line we go, "Gobble, gobble, gobble, gobble."

Joe: Then our band started to catch on. We will all be asleep, and they will all be like "Gobble, gobble." They are great guys.

# PLUG IN TO THE JONAS BROTHERS

Want to get in touch with Kevin, Joe, and Nick? Sure you do! Here are the best ways to reach out to the band of brothers . . .

Write to them c/o of their record company:

Jonas Brothers
c/o Hollywood Records
500 S. Buena Vista Street
Burbank, CA 91521

Write to them c/o of their TV channel:

Jonas Brothers
c/o The Disney Channel
3800 Alameda Ave.
Burbank, CA 91505

Write to them c/o of their fan club:

Jonas Brothers
P.O. Box 2567
Oak Ridge, NJ 07438

Or visit:
www.jonasbrothers.com

ROC